GUNNY

THE HYPERION SYSTEM

JACKI RAWLINSON

JRBooks.co.uk

GET IN TOUCH

Reach out to chat about the books:

Facebook - @authorjackirawlinson

Insta - @authorjackirawlinson

Website: www.jrbooks.co.uk

This story is based in the Hyperion System.

Also based in the Hyperion System is a series called 'The Emiliana Chronicles' - an

action-packed sci-fi space opera adventure!

Check it out here

The Emiliana Chronicles:

Book 1 - Emergence

Book 2 - Guardians Revenge

Book 3 - Raising R'avenn

Book 4 - Coming soon

The Hyperion System

Gunny - Out now on Amazon

T'imm - coming soon

Edraella - coming soon

Netwitch 1, 2, 3 - coming soon

INTRO FROM GUNNY

Hi. I've been asked to tell you a little about me or is that myself? Ah who cares anyway, I'm a Marine grunt. Not a damn college flake.

The name is Gunny. Ok, so that's not my name by birth. I'll tell you, but if you tell anyone else, I'll kick the living shit out of you, understood? My real name is Felicity Aurora Fairwether and I was born on Eskeron. I don't go by that name anymore, but that's another whole story. Before you ask, the answer is none of your goddamn business.

My mother was a pure J'ukkarian but not gifted. My father? Eskeron born and a Master Gunnery Sergeant in the Eskeron space marines. They died while out on a mission.

So after some time in the system, the authorities

handed me to a new military family when I was seven years old.

I am the youngest of four, having three older brothers. Two of them are marines, Gram and Lear, who accepted me into their family without too much drama and the other brother? Rex. An incorrigible bully and dropout. He was the bane of my life when I lived at home. He pulled humiliating pranks on me, teased me and beat me, any chance he got. That, combined with my father's strict military regulations and harsh discipline made my childhood a living hell. My so-called 'mother' was a mess, and clearly had her own baggage to contend with. We moved from base to base on various planets wherever my father was posted for the following five years.

When we were posted on Hoon, a gruelling five-day shuttle trip from Eskeron with my brothers, it was the first place I actually liked. The military school allowed me to begin combat and target practice at twelve years old, unlike some of the other military schools which restricted these sessions to over sixteens only. I owe Hoon Military School a lot. Not that Rex thought I should have anything to do with the military or combat. This only fuelled my determination to prove him and everyone else wrong. My stubbornness is my greatest strength and sometimes also my greatest enemy.

PLANET: HOON

MILITARY SCHOOL

Blood pumped through Felicity's ears as she focused on the target in front of her. She paused, took a breath and fired her weapon, hitting the moving target dead centre. She immediately fired off another four consecutive perfect shots, downing the remaining targets that popped out of random places in the training centre. She holstered her weapon and walked back to the hub to hydrate. She didn't smile or acknowledge what she had just achieved.

It had been another gruelling eight-hour session of running, combat, high-intensity circuits, target practice and repeat. Over and over. Each time a student was knocked out during combat, or missed a target they were disqualified. Felicity was the last woman standing. This had been the fourth time she had taken part in the sessions this month. Each time she succeeded, they put her up into the next age group's competition. She had just completed the course against the eighteen-year-olds.

"Shit, Felicity, you've just whooped the asses of all the sixth-year competitors…again. Aren't you even going to crack a smile?" Mark'Orr teased. He passed her a water pouch, allowing her to hydrate before she responded.

She glanced over to the Sergeant, ensuring he didn't see her talking with Mark'Orr. It was frowned upon to socialise with the lecturers. She shrugged, "It's no big deal, just want to get out of this shit hole. I'm ready. I've proven as much."

Mark'Orr was quite a few years older than Felicity. He graduated several years previously and was now a lecturer in the school, teaching Intel and Analysis.

Mark'Orr and Felicity struck a close friendship soon after she moved to Hoon with her adoptive family. Two loners, drawn together by their shared interest of solitude.

"It is a bit weird that you've completed the course more than once with a perfect score, yet they don't seem to want to acknowledge it." Mark'Orr went silent.

"Something stinks. There's bugger all I can do about it though. I'm going to get some fresh air." She sucked the last of the water from the pouch before tossing it in the waste receptacle. Mark'Orr watched Felicity's long strides as she exited the training complex. On the far side of the arena, he spotted Rex standing in the doorway, talking in hushed tones to the Military School Superintendent, Shona Williams. Mark'Orr frowned.

Mark'Orr casually sauntered to the exit. Once outside he caught up to Felicity as she marched down the path.

"So, Rex and Shona. What's going on there?" He asked as they walked.

"Shona, as in Superintendent Williams?" Felicity locked eyes with Mark'Orr.

"Yeah? I don't know any *other* Shona."

Felicity rolled her eyes at his sarcastic tone.

"What do you know then? Whatever it is, it's more than I know." She shrugged.

"Just saw them huddled in the doorway, talking quietly. Just seemed sus, that's all."

"Yeah. That does seem odd. Let me know if you spot them together again. Use those Intel skills you've been honing."

"Sure. I'll do what I can." He winked at her. "This is me," he nodded towards the Intel building to the right, where he taught the first-year kids. She didn't know where he found the patience to teach thirteen-year-olds.

"Catch you later Mark'Orr. I'm hitting the showers before my next class." Felicity waved casually as she headed for the shower block.

She lathered her shoulder-length hair, rinsing it through a couple of times, letting the hot water carry the suds over her tired body. She swallowed down the anger at being dismissed for the opportunity to go out on a mission. She knew she was ready. *Hell,* they *know I'm ready. So what if I'm sixteen? It's just a number, it means jack-shit.* She was so busy getting worked up that she didn't hear others entering the shower rooms until the noise levels had risen with all the horseplay. She turned the water off and grabbed her towel from the hook, rubbing the excess water from her body before squeezing the water out of her hair. She stepped out of the cubicle and groaned inwardly. *Ah just fucking great. This bunch of crap suckers is all I need.*

The largest of the group, Jerrid, nudged his friend beside him as they stood at the changing benches, already naked, standard-issue military towels wrapped around their waists.

"Look who we have here, boys. It's the one and only, Felicity Aurora Fairwether." His snarky tone ignited her anger. It was too similar to the tone her brother Rex used.

Felicity turned to walk to her locker.

"Fucking useless, is what you are. Rex told us all about you. Little fucking loner Felicity. You know they won't put you in the field because you'll never amount to anything. You're just a pair of legs and a whole lot of hot air. You'll probably be knocked up before school is out, if your mother is anything to go by." The group cracked up laughing.

Felicity faced them, "You know nothing. I just beat the lot of you in that arena today, and you're two years older than me. So maybe you should rethink who the useless ones are." As brave as she was, the comment about being useless still cut deep. She wasn't going to get into the details that the drunk woman was of no relation to her, as if that got back to her brothers, she'd get it from them. She desperately wanted to get out in the field. None of them knew who her real parents were. They only saw the fuck up of the family she was part of now. The family she was chained to, unwillingly.

"If you're so fucking great, then come on, bitch, show me what you've got." He taunted. She couldn't let it slide.

"You know that old saying, the bigger you are, the harder you fall? Well, you're going to demonstrate that to your buddies now," She smirked.

Jerrid steamed towards her like a freight train, throwing a haymaker at her face. It whistled past her nose as she subtly turned her head, dodging the clumsy blow.

"That all you got, big boy?" She taunted. Jerrid's friends visibly cringed.

That was a red rag to a bull, like she knew it would be. *So predictable.* She looked almost bored with his alpha male behaviour. He ran at her again and she sidestepped easily, allowing him to crash into the lockers, losing his towel in the process.

This failure only spurred his anger further.

"You stupid whore!" He spat out. He got up, forgetting his towel in his anger. He brought out his best moves, spinning around into a kick, positioning his fist ready for a second blow when she was down.

"Jerrid, stop!" One of his friends shouted. He was clearly the only one with a moral compass in the group as the others cheered him on. She pitied him for having so much faith in Jerrid being able to land a blow.

Felicity ducked low as his leg spun over her. She sprang up as his back was to her, grabbing his arm. In a quick twist and chop, she heard a distinctive crack. He howled out, turning to smack her with his other fist. As he turned, she focused all her strength into her palm, smacking him in the temple.

Knocked out cold, he hit the wet floor like a slab of rotten meat. Felicity glanced back at the rest of the group as she adjusted her towel.

"Come on then. Anyone else?" She fronted up to them.

They all stayed silent.

"No? Ok, get the fuck out of my way then." She growled as they parted when she stormed by.

Grabbing her pile of clothes, she opted to leave the shower blocks in her towel, rather than spend another second in that place. The cooler air hit her skin, causing a wave of goosebumps. Ignoring the frowns of the students nearby, Felicity marched in the direction of the residential lodges. When she arrived home, her bare feet were brown with dirt.

She ignored her poor excuse of a mother, who was passed out on the lounger. She marched to her room quickly to get dressed for the next lesson, which she knew she would now be late for, thanks to that scrotum rag, Jerrid.

"FELICITY. What do you think you are doing?" Her father's strict tone took her by surprise. She hadn't realised he was home. A feeling of dread filled her as she turned to face the man that she despised calling her father.

"I'm going to get dressed for my next lesson." She knew she shouldn't have spoken to him like that. But she didn't care at that moment. He approached at speed, slapping her across the face. She looked back at him defiantly.

"Address me properly," he demanded. He had always been this strict, from the day she was brought into their family. She remembered that her birth parents were strict too, from a military background, but they cared about her and showed her love. Now she had to put up with this less-than-savoury man.

"Sir, I am going to get dressed before my next lesson." Meeting his gaze directly.

"And what are you doing running around the campus in just a towel? You should be punished for such insolence. You will be late for your next class too. Another punishable offence." He looked at her expectantly. "Well?"

"There was a group in the shower rooms who attacked me. I acted in self-defence and had to leave the changing rooms before another fight started."

He grabbed her forearm roughly, pulling it towards him to inspect her.

"No marks. We shall see, Felicity. I am contacting Superintendent Williams to iron this out. If you have humiliated this family again, you will find yourself in serious trouble. Get out of my sight!" He barked.

Felicity turned to her bedroom, closing the door softly as she wiped a tear away. She slipped on her uniform, brushed her hair and left the house without a word.

2

PLANET: HOON

MILITARY SCHOOL

Mark'Orr watched from his vantage point at his desk, facing the window, as Felicity marched up the steps to the Intel and Analysis building. She was twenty minutes late for her lesson. A set of frown lines creased between her eyebrows. She looked upset and pissed off.

Mark'Orr pushed up from his desk and poked his head out of the classroom door.

"Felicity? You ok?" He whispered.

"Just fucking great. As usual." She scowled. "I'll talk to you later. Right now I'm late, another thing they'll hold against me."

The door at the end of the corridor swung open. Her furious year four lecturer frowned. His face reddened with anger.

"What time do you call this Felicity? Don't bother coming into my classroom. Go to Superintendent Williams. She is expecting you. And Mark'Orr? This is your *final* warning. Any more hanging around students will mean your suspension from teaching in this academy." He slammed the door in her face.

"Well, this is going to be a barrel of laughs." Felicity rolled her eyes and turned back for the exit.

"Hey, take no notice of him. I'll meet you later, you know where. We can catch up." Mark'Orr smiled at her before retreating into his empty classroom.

Felicity stormed out, ramming the door wide open. The sprung hinges creaked as they hit their limit, before swinging shut with a slam.

Superintendent Williams' office was on the other side of the campus. Felicity would no doubt be punished for being late, yet again.

Jogging along the path, she decided at the last minute to take a shortcut through the equipment store. Year fours weren't allowed in there, but at this point, she didn't give a damn.

She passed racks of ropes, balls, weights and other apparatus before getting to the door leading to an inner corridor. Poking her head out, she checked both ways before leaving the safety of the storage room. She was not looking forward to her meeting with Shona, or as she was supposed to call her 'Superintendent Williams'. The woman only ever acted out of her own best interests, no matter the cost or how it may affect others. Something Felicity despised.

She picked up the sound of two people talking. *Rex? Talking with Shona again are we?* She hung back around the corner, out of sight and listened intently.

"Yes, Shona-baby. I've made arrangements to send them a sample next week. If they like what they see, they'll come back for the lot," Rex's smarmy, arrogant tone grated Felicity.

"Ok, Rex, get it done. I want it finalised as soon as possible. There's a lot riding on this. And you won't see a credit until it's handed over to the Segurians," She snapped.

"I'm on it. Now, where's my kiss?" His smooth talk was weak and sickening.

"I don't have time for this Rex." She huffed. "Your sister is on her way here."

"What's that little rat gone and done now?" He asked, true hate in his voice.

Rat? He's the only rat on Hoon. Felicity clenched her fists. She was close to marching around the corner to tell him exactly what she thought of the wanker.

"Nothing for you to worry about. She'll get what's coming to her in time, don't worry."

"Good. The sooner the better. I've had to put up with the little bitch for too many years as it is."

"You better go." She snapped. Felicity heard feet shuffling, and she tensed, ready to sprint back down the hall. Listening carefully she heard a pair of heavily booted steps drift off in the other direction, while a feminine pair went into the office. As the door clicked shut, Felicity exhaled.

She was reeling from the exchange between Shona and Rex. *What the hell is going on? What are they giving to the Segurians? I have to speak to Mark'Orr tonight.*

"Here goes nothing." She mumbled as she turned the corner and marched to Shona's door. A shiny brass plaque sat proudly in the centre reading 'Superintendent Williams'.

Felicity knocked and waited.

"Enter." A nervous voice called.

Felicity stepped into the Superintendent's reception room, where a young graduate sat at a desk piled high with paperwork.

"Ms Fairwether, the Superintendent is waiting for you." He nodded her towards the door. Felicity tried not to roll her eyes at all this unnecessary fan fair. She knocked on Shona's door.

"Come in, Felicity," Shona called angrily. Felicity entered, closing the door behind her. She saluted the Superintendent, looking directly ahead, as she was trained. Shona was perfectly groomed and manicured as always. Opting for a tight-fitting non-military skirt suit to show off her curves.

Felicity stood, holding her salute, waiting to be released. Shona watched her silently. Felicity soon realised that she was being toyed with. Anger began to rise. *This woman and Rex belong together. Both are as evil as each other.* She seethed.

Shona rose from her chair, a smug look on her face, from what Felicity could see in her peripheral vision, or at least that's how she imagined her face must look at that moment. She walked past her desk and stood behind Felicity, just next to her ear.

"I've heard a few disturbing reports today about your behaviour. This school allowed you in, on the merits of your father and brothers who have all earned their respect on Hoon and served our military faithfully."

She paced the room behind Felicity. "We do *not* condone fighting outside of the combat ring. You know this. One of my most promising final-year students has reported to me that you attacked him, completely unprovoked. Yet he refused to break the oath, so he did not defend himself or retaliate." She came to stand in front of Felicity, too close for her liking. She could smell Rex's cologne and it made her stomach churn. Bringing up times from when she was younger.

Shona inspected Felicity's hands and face. She raised an eyebrow. "Not a scratch. Interesting. How did you manage to attack a year six student, breaking bones, yet there isn't a scratch on you? I think that is a testament to his statement. He clearly did not lay a finger on you."

Felicity couldn't hold her silence, "He attacked ME. I was the one who was defending myself." Before the slap even came, she knew she would get it once she uttered her final word. The sudden sting and heat on her left cheek shocked her even though she was mentally prepared for it. She continued to hold her salute, but was unable to control the tears forming in her eyes, simply from the harsh contact of Shona's palm on her face.

"You do *not* speak unless I say you can." Her tone was icy. "I have seen the evidence. I do not need you to comment on the matter. That is not what this is about." She gestured between herself and Felicity. "Your father called me and confirmed my suspicions, and then your Intel lecturer also alerted me that you were twenty minutes late for class." She began pacing again.

"Do you think this is some sort of clubhouse? Where you can prance around naked in jusr a towel, fight in the showers and fornicate with lecturers?" Felicity's eye's widened in shock.

What the fuck is she talking about?

"Oh, I know that look. Don't act all innocent and shocked with me. You and the Intel lecturer, Mark'Orr Derilin. I have seen the pair of you together. Yet another rule that is forbidden in this academy. Quite frankly, you don't seem to take anything that we do here seriously."

Felicity wanted to scream at this woman. She imagined pulling the bitches arm off and beating her with it until she passed out. She knew one of these days all the anger building up inside of her would explode out. Like an over-pressurised tube of squeezy cheese. It would never fit back in the tube again.

"I don't think you are committed to the military. I'm taking away your points from the tournaments you have won. And I am banning you from competing in future competitions. You have clearly just found an algorithm to beat the system anyway. How else could a year four student consecutively win against seasoned year six males? Ridiculous," She tittered.

"I am placing you under house arrest for the next three weeks. I want you to use this time to reflect on your behaviour. Perhaps you will see sense afterwards and prove to become useful to Hoon after all. Now get out of my sight!" She turned away, disinterested.

"Yes, Ma'am!" Felicity ground out, before quickly leaving the office and heading back to the campus grounds outside. Her face was red with anger as she stomped down the path.

How fucking dare she? I can't compete? Surely she knows Jerrid's reputation? Thoughts spun in her head like a washing machine. She nearly didn't hear Mark'Orr calling her as she marched along. She slowed to let him catch up.

"Oh shit. Are you ok? What happened?" He asked as he spotted the clear red handprint on her left cheek.

"I'm just fucking brilliant. Shona happened."

"Oh, shit."

"Yeah, you said that one already. We need to catch up, it's important."

"Ok. Come over to my class, it's empty now?"

"No, Shona has eyes on us. She thinks we are a 'thing.'"

"A thing?" He looked at her blankly. She rolled her eyes.

"A thing! Like, together." He still looked at her blankly.

"Seriously, you don't get it? She thinks we are fuck buddies." She noticed his cheeks colour up for a split second before he got himself under control.

"Ah, I see. Well, that's ok." He grinned.

"You wish. Anyway, meet me tonight, in the forest, you know the place."

"Ok, I have a late class at seven this evening. Is nine tonight ok?"

"Yeah, that should work for me. See you then. And find out everything you can on Segurians." She carried on marching down the path.

"Wait, what?" He called, confused about where that had come from or why she wanted to know about Segurians.

3

PLANET: HOON

Felicity quietly washed up the dishes, drying and packing them away as she went. Every clink of a bowl or cup had her cringing. She wanted as little attention on herself as possible. Her father had torn into her when she returned from Shona's office. She had a fat red welt on her arm to show for it.

"Goodnight mother, goodnight father," She called politely before padding down the hall and closing her door behind her. She hoped that by acting subservient, they would believe she felt sorry for what she did and leave her alone to contemplate her bad behaviour. She knew they would never take her word over Rex, Shona's or any other person on the base for that matter. She had given up imagining that they loved her many years ago. She was simply another source of income for them from the Hyperion Adoption Services.

She watched every agonising minute pass on the

clock as she listened to the movements of her parents in the living area down the hall. Her mother was drunk, as usual. Her father was on his way. Both would be passed out in front of the entertainment screen before long. That was their usual evening routine. Rex didn't usually come home to sleep at the weekends. And her two older brothers Gram and Lear had graduated a few years ago, so spent their time out on missions. Her coast would be clear.

As the clock hit 8:40 pm, she put a pillow inside her covers and turned off her bedroom light. She slid the window across and climbed out as quietly as she could. A new creak sounded in the boards outside her window as she placed her foot down. She froze, waiting to see if her father heard. No footsteps. She pulled her other leg out easily, quietly thanking her birth parents for her long legs right now. Sliding the window shut, she covered her blonde hair with the hood of her jacket.

She crunched down the gravel path, trying to look as inconspicuous as possible. Once she entered the forest, she relaxed slightly. The darkness enveloped her, allowing her to walk casually without the worry of being spotted.

She enjoyed the sound of little insects clicking and buzzing as she strolled along, thinking about everything Rex and Shona had discussed. It was all she could focus on. The punishment, the not being able to compete; these things pissed her off, but were out of her control.

She now had something she could focus on while she

was in isolation. Felicity was stubborn to her core. She marched along, immersed in mulling over possible solutions.

At the crunch of leaves to her right, she smiled, looking up to greet Mark'Orr. Instead, what greeted her was a heavy thud in the face, loss of vision, and ringing in her ears as she fell to the ground. She felt disorientated as she scrabbled to her knees. "What the…" Her head swam and her vision blurred. She could see multiple people surrounding her. They were laughing and jeering.

Oh shit, as she started to regain her senses, she was knocked down again with a second blow to the side of the head. She lay on her side groaning. A pair of hands roughly pushed her onto her back, as another pair held her legs down.

"So little bitch. It's payback. You didn't think I'd just let you get away with it, did you?" There was zero humour in his tone. Only the sound of a bitter and twisted young man. Just the kind of guy that Superintendent Williams seemed to like.

Felicity could barely speak she was still recovering from the injury to her head. She remembered her training and tried to take in any details she could. She thought there were three guys. Jerrid and two others. She mentally prepared herself for a beating. Her brother and father hit her often, so she was sure she'd had enough training in that area.

All her preparation went out the window when she heard the clink of a flick knife, and the rip of her military-issue trousers. She pushed up with her knees, unable to move. She earned herself a kick in the ribs.

"Fuck you, Jerrid," she spat at where she guessed he was. He growled so she assumed she hit her mark.

"Just you wait, little bitch. You'll be knocked up before the end of the night, your destiny set out for you, just like I said." The other two laughed as she heard a belt buckle. She thrashed wildly, screaming with all her power. A blood curdling sound like she had never made before.

"Shut the bitch up!" Jerrid scowled, before everything went black.

A series of booms echoed in Felicity's mind. She groaned as she tried to peel her eyes open. Everything hurt. The sounds around her grew louder as she gained consciousness.

"FELICITY! Fuck. Felicity! Get up!" A voice urged her.

Is that Mark'Orr? What the hell is going on? Everything came back to her in a flash of images. *Jerrid.* She sat up instantly, ignoring the pain in her head, ribs and other areas. She felt a wave of nausea. Her one eye was sealed shut, she guessed from the smack in the face. She focused on Mark'Orr who was right in front of her.

"Mark… what the hell…" She took a breath. Trying to detach her body from her mind to deal with what may have happened. "I thought it was you, but it was them." She was pissed at herself for being so distracted and not hearing three people ambush her. She glanced down at her battered, naked body as Mark'Orr slid his jacket off and wrapped it around her shoulders.

"Come on. We need to get out of here. Think you can try to walk if I help you?" Felicity could hear the panic in Mark'Orr's voice. He was in shock too. She had to be strong. This was not the time to flake out on him. Her one friend.

She nodded, putting on a brave face. "Yes. I think so."

Mark'Orr stepped behind her to help lift her from under her arms. Felicity winced, unable to hold it in.

"Shit. Sorry. I can carry you?" He offered.

"No. I can walk. Where are we going? I think I have some broken bones, and I'm not sure what else is damaged." Her voice came out in a pant from the amount of pain she was in. She glanced back down at herself. She looked like she had been dunked in a blood bath, and rolled in leaves. Her head swam dizzily.

"We can't go to the sick bay. I'm taking you somewhere else." He stood beside her, putting her arm over his shoulder to support her.

Felicity looked around in the pitch-black. As her eyes adjusted, she could make out three figures laid out on the damp ground.

"Mark'Orr, what about them?" She pointed to her attackers. "Shona won't believe that I'm innocent, even with my injuries."

Mark'Orr shook his head, the moonlight showed his pale skin and worried expression. "They won't be a problem anymore, Felicity. We need to get out of here." He guided her away from the clearing, into the darkness. For once she had no clever retort or anything to say.

"I need to stop for a minute," Felicity croaked out.

Mark'Orr stopped, taking her full weight. "Not long now, just another hundred metres and we'll be there." He reassured her. She nodded, not wanting to seem weak, but her head felt like it was ten times heavier than it should be. She was sure she had lost a substantial amount of blood. She began analysing what had happened, but it only made her panic. Her DNA was all over that area. She was in deep shit if Mark'Orr had really killed those three. She would never admit his involvement though.

They passed what felt like the same set of trees for the third time before the forest became sparse, opening up to a field and just off to the right, a small green shed sat on its own. Mark'Orr pointed at it.

"Nearly there."

"We're going to hide in a shed?" Felicity slurred and giggled. The pain and adrenaline was doing something to her.

Mark'Orr looked sideways at her, knowing that for her to giggle she definitely wasn't right in the head.

"No. That's ridiculous. Just come." He helped her to the shed, letting her lean against the side while he fumbled with a code lock. He swung the pair of old doors open, the hinges creaked in distress, before he disappeared inside.

Felicity jumped when she heard something chugging out. It was an old-style electric quad bike.

"Wow, is this yours?" She asked.

"Not exactly." He answered cryptically. She decided not to press for more details, and it was just too much effort in her current state.

Mark'Orr jumped off, locked the shed and came back to lift Felicity onto the bike. He was aware of her injuries, so helped her to sit on the parcel shelf at the back. It was the best he could do.

"You holding on? Think you'll be ok back there?" He asked.

"Yeah, I think so. No idea where we are going. But let's get there. I think I'm going to pass out soon," She mumbled as her head lolled.

"Shit. Ok," He accelerated, glancing over his shoulder every minute to make sure he hadn't lost her off the back of the bike.

They stayed off-road, to ensure they weren't spotted by anyone. Mark'Orr tried to navigate around the roughest terrain to save Felicity additional pain as she perched on the parcel shelf of the quad. They had been travelling for thirty minutes when he pulled out of the forest and onto an old, overgrown dirt track. This

23

meandered uphill someway until they parked up outside an old log cabin. The lights were on inside.

"Is this it?" Felicity asked weakly from her slumped position on the back of the bike. She really hoped this was not just another stop-off.

"Yeah. This is it, Flick." He reassured, calling her by a nickname he hadn't used since they were children. He jumped off. Scooping Felicity up easily, he marched up the steps and gently booted the door three times, paused then booted it another two times.

After a moment, the door opened a crack.

"Mark'Orr? What the fuck?" A man with a strange accent asked as he opened the door wider.

"Can I come in, Kavvin?" He asked urgently.

"What's in it for me?" Kavvin countered.

Mark'Orr sighed, "I think she has some information you could use. But first, she needs help."

"Ah fuck. What kind of trouble are you dragging me into? You weren't followed were you?" He ushered them in as he scanned the grounds outside.

"No, we weren't followed. But there is a bit of a mess in the forest near the campus that needs cleaning up. Think you have anyone that can help?"

"Put her down there. Let's get her stable, then you need to tell me exactly what's happened so that I can see if it's something I can help you with." Kavvin traded in information. It was his business. That was how he met Mark'Orr some years ago. Mark'Orr knew that Kavvin was helping him, but at the same time, he was fishing for information that he could use to benefit himself. He didn't blame the guy, that was how he made his living nowadays. Mark'orr knew Kavvin was a good guy.

He placed Felicity on the table, as Kavvin swiped a lumpy cushion from the armchair to place under her head, and draped an old throw over her for modesty. Mark'Orr watched as her eyes closed, unable to stay awake any longer. He stepped away from the table, motioning for Kavvin to come closer.

"I was meant to meet Felicity in the forest tonight, as she has been in some trouble with the Superintendent after a fight with some year six students. She must have overheard something, I'm sure of it because she was rambling on about the Segurians after she mentioned that she'd been put on a 3 week three-week isolation from school. She asked me to find out some information on Segurians and to meet her in the forest to talk about it. Anyway, so earlier tonight I headed to the place we usually meet, and I heard a lot of shouts and scuffling. I saw three large figures holding her down. I just saw red. I shot all three of them." He stepped over to check Felicity's vitals.

"What, so you just happened to have a weapon on you, seeing as Intelligence Lecturers are always armed while they stroll around campus?" Kavvin snorted.

Mark'Orr rolled his eyes. "No, I had my plasma pistol on me, as I was going to do some target practice in the woods with Felicity. It's kind of a tradition. It's not military issue."

"Ooh, naughty boy, carrying unlicensed weapons on campus!" He smirked.

"Listen I really need your help. I know that people don't generally go into that area of the forest, so I'm sure the bodies won't be discovered anytime soon. Think we can try to make it look like a shootout, between the three of them? …We need to wipe them of Felicity's DNA."

"Shit man, that is a lot to ask. The bastards clearly deserved it looking at what they did to the girl though," He paused scratching his long black unwashed hair.

"If we don't, they'll trace it back to her and blame her for it." Mark'Orr shook his head.

"Ok. But the information the girl has better be worth it. I'll have to go make some calls." They both looked up as Felicity's battered body began to convulse from a seizure.

"Shit. I'll get the med kit. Turn her on her side!" He ordered as he sprinted into the kitchen. Mark'Orr held her on her side, ignoring the foamy saliva pouring from her mouth, as he rubbed her back.

Felicity's seizure slowed and stopped, but Mark'Orr had no idea if she could recover from this. She had lost a huge amount of blood, probably had a series of internal injuries and severe head trauma.

Shit. What have I done? I should have taken her to the medical room on campus. If anything happens to her it's on me. He felt himself get hot with panic.

Kavvin returned with a medkit and another smaller black box which he held close to him.

"What's that?" Mark'Orr pointed at the box.

"This might be the only thing that saves your friend's life. If I use this, you owe me. Big time. This is worth more than six years of earnings."

"Whatever the cost. Just do it. She *can't* die." He urged.

"Ok, just sign this," He held out his comm device, the screen showing a signature box.

"Are you fucking kidding? My friend is dying and you want me to sign something to say I owe you?"

"Tick-tock. You're the one wasting time here," Kavvin tapped the screen. Mark'Orr reached over and signed his name, and clicked submit. A second screen popped up asking him to place his left index finger on the screen and look into the camera. He scowled up at Kavvin before following the instructions.

"Submission complete," a feminine electronic voice announced.

"Ok, do it. Save her!" Mark'Orr barked. It was unlike him to get angry, but he was getting desperate.

Kavvin clicked the little case open, a single metal injector sat nestled in foam, alongside a vial of bright green liquid.

"Lift the blanket, it needs to go into her thigh, in the main artery."

"What? Why can't you just do it in her arm?"

"Trust me, it's the quickest and safest way. Unless you want me to go through her chest bone, and risk further injury."

"Fuck. Just do it," Mark'Orr lifted the blanket,

exposing Felicity's long creamy coloured legs, now covered in blood and bruises.

Kavvin slotted the vial into the top of the injector. It clicked into place piercing the seal. Leaning over the table, he placed a hand on her knee, sliding it up her thigh as he estimated the rough position of where her artery should be.

Mark'Orr didn't like Kavvin putting his hands on her, but he kept his mouth shut, knowing he was only trying to help.

Kavvin used a pointer finger to mark the place where he intended to inject.

"Pass me that pen." He pointed to the side table next to the armchair.

Mark'Orr rifled through the pile of crap on the table before finally finding the pen and passing it to Kavvin.

Kavvin marked the spot and discarded the pen, chucking it over his shoulder.

"Ok, here it goes. If this doesn't work, I still tried. This shit is valuable."

"Do it!" Mark'Orr ordered.

Kavvin slammed the injector into her thigh, hitting the pen mark accurately. The green liquid disappeared from the clear vial at the top, entering Felicity's bloodstream.

Before he'd had a chance to take the injector out, she gasped and sat upright, smacking the injector away from her leg. She immediately passed out again. Falling back to the table. Mark'Orr managed to grab her shoulders before she sustained further injury to her skull.

"Check her breathing and heart," Kavvin recommended.

Mark'Orr leaned in close. Her hot breath came out rhythmically as if she was in a deep, relaxing sleep. Her heart rate sounded strong and even. He looked up at Kavvin and nodded. "I think she's ok." He wiped the sweat from his brow using his forearm.

"Let's get her into bed. She can have my room. She will need to sleep it off now."

Mark'Orr pulled Kavvin into a manly hug, slapping him once on the back. "Thank you. Thank you." He returned to Felicity's side and began assessing her other injuries from top to toe, cleaning her up as best as he could.

4

PLANET: HOON

KAVVIN'S CABIN

Pain thrummed through Felicity's body. She opened her one good eye to take in her surroundings. She was in a bed. On the wall above her were strange weapons and ornate carved pieces depicting a variety of creatures. The first thing she realised was that this was not her bed. She tried to sit up, but a hand on her shoulder stopped her, pushing her back down. She panicked for a second at the feeling, before locking her eye on Mark'Orr.

"Hey. You're awake. I'd stay flat for a while longer. I've had to stitch up the worst of your cuts, and I think we need to let your body heal a bit," He spoke quietly.

"You look like shit," She croaked. He smiled.

"Thanks. Ditto, Flick."

Gunny swallowed then cleared her throat, "Last night. That was Jerrid, and two of his friends." Mark'Orr nodded, allowing her to continue. "We fought earlier in the day in the shower rooms. Well, I say we fought. I let him make a fool of himself and then I broke his arm. But Williams took his word over mine. Before I got to her office though, I overheard her talking with Rex about Segurians and some deal."

"Are you sure you're ok to talk about this now, after what you have just been through last night?"

"Yes. I need to tell you. It's important." She insisted.

"Ok, would you mind if I call Kavvin in?"

"Sure." She nodded. "But how does this interest him?"

"He deals in buying and selling information. That's how he makes his living these days. He knows everything that goes on. That's how we crossed paths years ago. Me being me, poking my nose in business that had nothing to do with me was how I came across Kavvin. That story is for another time. Right now, the topic is the Segurians. I fucking hate those space pirates." Mark'Orr stood from his chair beside the bed, and poked his head out the door, calling Kavvin into the room.

"Hey, Kav. We're ready to figure out what's going on with the Segurians." Mark'Orr invited Kavvin in.

"Good to see you are awake, Felicity and have some colour back in your cheeks. I hope you are finding my room comfortable?"

"Thank's for helping me. Both of you. What will happen to the bodies of the three who attacked me? Surely if they're found, the alarm will be raised, as we are missing?"

"We sorted that last night. They were moved to a new site in the forest, closer to their own accommodations. It now looks like they were having a bit of fun on a shootout. And happened to be carrying illegal plasma pistols. Naughty Naughty." Kavvin waggled his eyebrows at Mark'Orr.

"Shit-a-brick. Hope Williams doesn't go sniffing any further then," Felicity croaked out, cringing.

"Right. Tell me about the Segurians, what do you know?" Kavvin pressed.

"Well, my brother Rex and Superintendent Shona? Definitely together in some capacity, although it sounds like she is just using him as a go-between with the Segurians. He is just arrogant enough to believe she really does want him. I overheard them talk about getting a sample to the Segurians, and if they liked it, they would purchase a mass order."

"A sample? Hmm." Kavvin scratched his head.

"Can it be a weapon?" She watched his face as he thought about it.

"No, I don't think so. The Segurians have quite a range of weapons they've acquired on the dark market. There is something else though. You heard of GSET?" Kavvin asked the pair.

"Fuck. Isn't that the Gene Shock Enhancement therapy that's issued to special ops teams on Eskeron who are assigned to high-profile missions?" She sat up before Mark'Orr could push her back down. She winced as her skin pulled taught in places.

"Exactly. It makes them stronger, faster, better," Kavvin gazed at Felicity.

"If that's what they're planning. We need to stop them," Mark'Orr insisted.

"Mark, no one will believe us. Trust me, especially Shona, she is batting for another team entirely. No matter what I say, she would twist it to suit her needs." He nodded in understanding.

"There is only one way we can stop them." A glint returned to her eyes. As the other two locked their gaze with her one eye.

"We will have to intercept the transaction. Get proof." She suggested. "But we can't take that proof to anyone on Hoon. We need a higher power. Mark'Orr, surely you have contacts on Eskeron. You said your parents were from there?"

A look of pain passed over Mark'Orr's face, but he quickly recovered. "Yes, I am in contact with the Central Eskeron Military Base occasionally. Let me look into it and see who could be a trustworthy person to report to."

"Mark'Orr, I suggest you also do some digging into when and where these transactions might be taking place. We want the big transaction, not the sample," Kavvin suggested as he stood. "Ok. Felicity, I think you need to rest, I'll bring you some food in a bit."

"Think I can have a shower?" She asked.

"Sure, it's right next door to this room. I've put some clothes on the chest there. Sorry, that's all I had spare, so they might be a bit big on you. I'll make sure there's a towel in the washroom for you."

"That's ok. Thank you."

Mark'Orr and Kavvin left Felicity, closing the door behind them.

Felicity pulled the covers back, revealing a range of scratches and bruises on her legs. She was wearing a large old t-shirt that had some sort of furry creature emblazoned on the front. She swung her legs out of the bed and winced slightly. Pain radiated through her from various places on her body. She wished she could exact revenge on Jerrid for what he did to her. At least he was no longer able to breathe the oxygen of Hoon ever again. Thinking about what he did to her made her want to vomit. Bile rose up into her throat and she swallowed, squeezing her eyes shut for a moment.

She wanted to scrub everything from yesterday out of her mind. She *needed* to if she wanted to hold onto her sanity. Anger bubbled up at the thought of Jerrid, Rex, Shona and her adoptive father. None of these people were good. *Why can't anyone else see it? Why hasn't anyone tried to fight back? I can't let her get away with whatever she has up her sleeve. What is her game plan? How many students is she manipulating to get what she wants?*

Felicity stood up, letting the pain fuel her to move. She was surprised she didn't feel worse. She shuffled out of the bedroom, grabbing the clothes folded on the side as she left, heading into the main living area. Kavvin nodded to her. He sat on a wooden chair at the table where she lay last night, half-naked. He went back to his screen, tapping away. She cringed at the thought. She wanted no one to know about this. Ever. If she could wipe it from their memories she would.

In the washroom, she took off the oversized t-shirt and turned on the hot water. Stepping in, she stood under the spray, letting the water envelope her body. Reddy-brown blood swirled in with the water and down the drain. She gently rubbed her head, knowing she had been hit there multiple times. She was scared of what injuries she might find. With her fingertips, she massaged through her hair, starting at her ears, and working her way up.

What? Where are the stitches? Felicity couldn't find any injuries. She picked up the small bar of soap and lathered it between her hands before leaning over and washing her legs. She felt a lump on her thigh. On closer inspection, it had a set of three small holes in the centre. Then a flashback of her on the table came to mind. She had seen something stuck in her leg. It stung and she batted it away. She couldn't remember anything after that. *What was it that they injected me with? Is that why I don't feel too bad today?*

She quickly washed her hair and the rest of her body before turning off the water and getting dry.

Staring at herself in the small steamy mirror she grimaced. *I need a change. That isn't me anymore.*

Rummaging in the small mirrored cabinet, she found a comb. She examined her face in the mirror as she brushed out the knots in her hair. Now that the dried blood was washed away, she couldn't see any wounds, just a few pale bruises. "How is this possible?" She muttered. She opened the cabinet again and grabbed the scissors and a shaving blade.

"Here goes nothing." She started snipping the ends of her hair. Each time chopping more and more. She neatened up her do with a razor. "Hell yes, bitch," She nodded, pleased with her new look.

She pulled on the clothes Kavvin had lent her. The tracksuit bottoms were black and quite large. Her long legs fit them perfectly. She pulled the waist cord tight, tying it in a knot. Unfolding the t-shirt she let out a snort. "What is it with Kavvin and these fucking furry creatures?" She muttered, sliding the t-shirt over her head.

As she left the washroom, Mark'Orr looked at her and stood in surprise.

"Shit. You're up. Your hair. How're you feeling?" He asked, clearly still worried about her and surprised by her new haircut.

"Hi, what is this, question time?" She smiled weakly. "I feel ok. They did a number on me, and really I should be feeling worse than I do, but I actually feel super energised. And the hair? This is the new me. The Felicity of yesterday is no more. Fuck. I hate that name." She noticed Mark'Orr glance at Kavvin and nod.

"Want to tell me what's going on? What was that injection you gave me last night? It left a nice looking welt on my thigh." She looked between the two men.

"I brought you here last night and asked Kavvin to

36

help me. He had some medicine that he said could save your life. I didn't ask questions, I just told him to give it to you. We nearly lost you." He looked away, hiding his emotions.

"Thank you Kavvin," Felicity wasn't good with feelings and hated when things got mushy. It looked like Kavvin felt the same as he waved her off.

"Ah, it's *Markyboy* here you should be thanking, he has pretty much signed himself up for anything I ask for as payment," He grinned.

"Must be good shit. What is it?" She asked.

Kavvin gulped before he answered, "It was a sample of GSET…"

5

PLANET: HOON
KAVVIN'S CABIN

"You shot me up with GSET?!" Felicity looked at Kavvin in disbelief. She rubbed the back of her neck, feeling the shaved hair.

"Well yeah. I've seen it in action. Brings people back from the brink. I knew it would do the trick," He waved her off casually.

"You told me there was a chance it wouldn't work?" Mark'Orr eyeballed Kavvin.

"Well, there's always a risk with anything medical. Every species may have different reactions. But Felicity here looks like she is mostly Eskeron, so I figured she'd be ok."

"You realise she's also half J'ukkarian?" Mark'Orr blurted before glancing back at Felicity. He knew she didn't like people knowing about her past. She was an extremely private person.

Kavvin perked up. "Ah, is this so? Interesting," He grinned. "Not a gifted by any chance?"

Felicity shook her head, "No, my mother was in the military on J'ukkar, she fought alongside those that were gifted. Care to share what you are finding so interesting?" Felicity asked impatiently.

"Just that GSET is, as you know, used to enhance soldiers. But it has also been used as a way to bring the fatally wounded back into the safety zone so that they can recover. Each shot contains a variety of ingredients along with a dose of nanites. The range of effects of GSET has only ever been proven on Hoon and Eskeron soldiers. J'ukkarian blood is untested as far as I know."

"So, I could keel over at any point from these unknown side effects?" Felicity probed, ensuring she showed no fear in front of Kavvin.

"Hold on now, I think you are being a bit dramatic. Clearly it did its job in bringing you back. Trust me when I say you were in a *very* bad way last night. Just the external injuries alone were enough of a worry. Who knows what internal injuries you suffered, gauging by the bruising and wounds you sustained. Just before we gave you the shot, you were convulsing. The head injuries and mass amount of blood loss were taking their toll. The nanites helped with the healing, along with some other unknown ingredients that seem to shock your DNA, making it evolve."

"So we have nothing to worry about?" Mark'Orr interrupted. Felicity realised he must feel responsible.

"Before you both get your knickers in a twist, I don't think there's anything to worry about," Kavvin reassured. "I would be interested to see if the shot has affected you in any other way though. Tomorrow we'll do some simple training exercises to test your reflexes and ensure you are healed. Mark'Orr tells me you are quite the fighter?" He smiled at her.

"I just do what I have to do. I don't care about winning those tournaments, I just wanted to prove that I was ready to be assigned to off-planet missions. They seem to feel I am not mission-material."

"Felicity, I think that has more to do with your brother and father's influence than anything else."

"Nice to know I'm not the only one with a fuck tonne of baggage." Kavvin laughed but soon realised the other two were not laughing along with him.

"I think we all need something to eat. I'm not used to having people over. Sit tight, I'll heat up some of the soup I have in the freezer for us." Kavvin disappeared into the kitchen.

"Mark, how long are we staying here? I feel like we are imposing." She sat down on the tatty, old two-seater. Mark'Orr crossed the room and sat down beside her.

"Well I need to gather some more information, but I guess until we can get evidence on Shona and anyone else she is linked with, we need to stay hidden."

"Won't they be looking for us? Shona, my father and brother?"

"Yeah probably. Even more reason to stay hidden, the

only reason they would want to find us, is to pin more on us. We have no allies on campus. I expect after the previous accusations from Shona, that she assumes we quit campus life and ran off together."

"You're right there. Shit. I'm sorry to have dragged you into this whole mess," Gunny rubbed her temples.

"You're my friend. I wasn't about to leave you."

"So, did you know that Kavvin had GSET here?" She watched Mark'Orr's expression change from calm to stressed.

"No," He looked down.

"So, what would have happened if...," Mark'Orr stopped her mid-sentence.

"I don't want to think about that, ok? I didn't know what to do. I'd just killed three students and witnessed a brutal attack. I was panicking and needed to get to the only other person on Hoon that I trust." That shut Felicity up.

"I'm sorry Mark'Orr. It must've been tough on you. Are you ok? You know, after the shooting. I can't imagine how you are feeling right now."

"It's strange. The killing part doesn't actually bother me. If they had been good people, perhaps it might've. The thing that bothered me most is what they did to you. How they treated you," He gulped.

"Listen, Mark." Felicity put a hand on his knee. Not a gesture she had done many times. "I just want to forget about yesterday. Can we make an agreement that we never talk about it again? Ever?"

She stressed her last word. A look of desperation in her eyes.

Mark'Orr gazed at her perfect blue eyes, reading her emotions and body language. She was being open and honest with him. He knew he would do anything for her, and if this is what she wanted. Then so be it. "Ok. Deal. But if you ever change your mind, and want to talk, you know you can trust me. Even though I know you hate all that emotional stuff." He rolled his eyes.

She spat in her hand and held it out, "Shake on it?"

He spat in his own hand, slapping it to hers in a firm shake. He hoped this was the right thing for her. He knew her well enough not to press her on matters she didn't want to discuss.

Felicity cracked open her eyes, the swelling had gone down completely now, and she could see clearly. She stretched and got out of bed. "No pain. Thank you, GSET," She mumbled as she got dressed. A note was stuck to the door.

Morning.
Come outside for a training session when you are up and dressed. I will be waiting for you out the back. Training on an empty stomach is better for you.
Kavvin

She left in search of Kavvin. Walking around the back, where the forest was much denser. She stopped, glancing left and right when she heard a rustle in the trees. Looking up, she spotted him.

"Morning! Are you ready Felicity?" Kavvin called from his perch in the trees.

"Ready for what?" She called grouchily.

"To test your skills with the master?" He laughed.

"Master? Of what? Making soup and stealing information?"

"Oh, you do jest, young Felicity," He smiled as he easily hopped from one branch to the next until he landed gracefully on the floor with barely a sound. She nodded, impressed.

"First a warm-up. Jog to that far tree, across and then back. Repeat four times."

Felicity looked down at her bare feet. "I don't have any boots?"

"Are you a soldier or a little bitch?" He laughed. She ignored him and started jogging. She felt incredible, her legs felt powerful like she could run forever.

After the fourth lap, she returned. "So what next?"

"Tell me how you felt?"

"I felt like I could just keep going." She smiled.

"And now tell me what you did wrong?" He looked at her expectantly. Felicity looked at him blankly and shrugged. "You don't know? Ok, you sounded like a herd of Ocillon, stampeding through the forest. You must always be aware. Aware of yourself and aware of your surroundings. That needs to be second nature."

"I don't even want to know what an Ocillon is. Where did you learn this stuff anyway? What did you do before you lived in this cabin?"

"The furball on your t-shirt is an Ocillon. They are not a creature to be messed with." He pointed at her in warning, his bright green eyes piercing her with his gaze. "I'm half Alorean and half Hoon. My mother was from Hoon, and my father was from Alorea. He met her on a peacekeeping mission and took her back to Alorea with him. I was born on Alorea and learnt their ways until I came of age. They are very traditional on Alorea and didn't want a half-blood in their circles. No pure-blood Alorean would have black hair. My father's family shunned me. My mother and I left Alorea. She settled back on Hoon and I got mixed up with a Mercenary ship for some years after. Finally, I'd had enough of that, so I decided to buy myself a little plot out here in the middle of nowhere to retire."

"Shit. Ok. I've heard a bit about Aloreans. You guys definitely know how to fight." She realised that she would have to ignore the long, greasy, black hair, scruffy clothes and unshaven jaw. She should know by now that looks could be deceiving.

"Glad you realise this. So you should be grateful that I feel like sharing some of my knowledge with you."

"Oh, so it's only because you're feeling charitable and

has nothing to do with the fact that you gave me GSET and now you want to treat me like your very own little experiment?" She raised an eyebrow at him.

"Yeah, maybe a bit of that too. But either way, it's a win-win for you." She couldn't argue with that. "Later, I want you to practice awareness. Let the sounds around you be heard, but you must be able to disappear into those sounds. Attacks like the one you experienced the other night will never happen again if you are always prepared and always fully aware of your surroundings. Now we will practice speed and agility. Fighting stance please."

"Ok. But, Kavvin, just so you know, I don't want to discuss the attack. I just want to move forward." Kavvin nodded, a momentary glint of sadness in his eyes. Felicity rolled her neck, facing him. Knees slightly bent, in a relaxed posture. She nodded to show she was ready.

He smacked her to the floor before she realised what had hit her.

"Fuck!" She was pissed at herself. "How are you so fast?"

"It must be all the years of training five hours a day. That and the Alorean blood probably helps a bit too."

"Ok, well I'm ready this time. I wasn't sure what to expect, so you caught me off guard." She grumbled.

"Exactly and that's why I mention not just being strong and having good practical skills, but having a sixth sense of awareness. Ready." He faced her and bowed.

Felicity took a breath and focused, zoning in on Kavvin. As he moved, it was as if she had adjusted his speed in her mind, she could see his subtle changes in stance as he was about to spin and kick at her. She easily ducked, grabbing his leg and pulling him to the ground as everything came back to full speed again.

"Ha! Excellent. Quite extraordinary. I can see you are a good fighter already, but tell me, what do you feel was different this time, compared to when you usually fight?" Kavvin looked at Felicity proudly. The look of surprise on her face told him the GSET was working wonders.

"Everything slowed down. I focused like you said, and I was able to see your movements happen with plenty of time to plan a countermove."

Kavvin clapped his hands like an excited child. "Now let's combine speed and accuracy with a series of consecutive manoeuvres."

The days went on like this, as Felicity gained confidence. She picked up many of Kavvin's Alorean tricks. Combined with the effects of the GSET, she was even more of a force to be reckoned with.

"Felicity, Kavvin, come over here," Mark'Orr called from his spot at the table, behind two large screens he had rigged up.

The pair moved to watch over his shoulder as he motioned towards the screens.

"I started checking all the current projects that Shona has open, to see if there was any mention of GSET or a transfer. I have been hitting brick walls for the past few days. Until today. See these codes?" He pointed at a series of codes on a diagram. "Well I've cross-referenced every code in the diagram of all the open projects, and these ones don't actually link to the project database. They are completely random. So I'm sure you can guess what that means?" Kavvin and Felicity glanced at each other and shrugged.

"Well, I decided to run some algorithm checks on these number sequences. It's a code!" They've been communicating through code in this string of numbers on the diagrams. Very clever," He smiled.

"I don't get it. Why would she do that?" Felicity asked impatiently.

"So that if the messages being sent out were intercepted, they would appear to simply be project plans for upcoming student training sessions or tactical mission training. A boring document that no one would be interested in."

"Come on then, tell us already, what does the code mean?" Kavvin sat down beside Mark'Orr.

"I have been able to figure out most of it, but only a few of the digit sequences don't convert when I run them through my program." He pointed to a small window in the bottom right of the screen as he pasted the codes.

Text appeared in the results box, Kavvin and Felicity leaned forward to read it.

A GSET sample transfer is to take place on the third day of the second month at sunset on Hoon time.

"But that was last week!" Felicity slammed her fist on the table but quickly pulled her hand back when Kavvin looked at her accusingly.

"Yes, I know. The second numbers must have been coded slightly differently as I am unable to decode them quite so accurately. Here, take a look." He pasted the next set of numbers into the program, it was a tense few seconds for the three, as it translated them. The results popped up in the box with a small chime. Silence followed as Kavvin and Felicity read the decoded message.

*A fu*1L sh9ment 0f GzE*7 2 b3 x*fered. 2 tyke pl*4ce on th3 31*ghtth d4y 0f s*th 1rd m0nth at 3*rty past 1L*8 pM H0*th t1m*3.*

"What the hell does that say?" Felicity almost banged the table a second time but decided against it under Kavvin's watchful gaze.

"Well, if we break it down, I think it says something like a full shipment of GSET to be transferred. To take place on the… I think that says the eighth day of the third month at… 3 past or thirty past 8 pm, Hoon time," Mark'Orr scratched his head as he re-read the half-decoded message.

Kavvin stood up suddenly. "Eighth day of the third month! That's in two days' time!"

"We need to stop them. We can clear our names and also stop this GSET from getting into the hands of the Segurians and who knows who else they'll sell it on to."

"How can we stop them?" Mark'Orr threw his hands up.

"Simple." Felicity put her hands behind her back as she paced around the table, formulating a plan. "If we get there early enough, we can find a spot to hide out, then when the Segurians are about to take possession of the goods, we can alert the security of the pirate's presence on Hoon, and about the illegal transaction taking place. They'll swoop in and stop the transaction. Shona Williams will get arrested, as will anyone she is linked with," Felicity nodded to herself.

"Who is going to believe *us*?" Mark'Orr snorted. Felicity snapped her head back around.

"Your contacts in Eskeron?" She suggested, raising an eyebrow as if that was obvious.

Mark'Orr groaned. "We need to do this. It's our only chance to clear our names and allow us to be taken seriously."

"Well, it's not your only option." Kavvin interrupted from his place at the table. Mark'Orr and Gunny locked eyes with him, waiting for him to continue.

"I have contacts too and people always owe me favours." He waggled his eyebrows. "I could get you onto the merc ship, you could run missions with the crew. They are a good bunch if you look past their fucked up lives and values."

Felicity looked at Kavvin as if he had three heads.

"As nice as your offer is, I am going to have to decline. I *will* be part of the Eskeron Military. It is what my true parents would have wanted. It's what I fucking want. This is the only route to take. We need to catch the Segurians red-handed." Felicity's tone was serious. Kavvin nodded.

"Ok, I'm in. I'll help you get as far as the border of the airfield - assuming that is where they are landing." Kavvin offered.

"Thank you Kavvin. You have done so much for us already, taking us in and helping Felicity. Please don't feel you have to come along." Mark'Orr patted his friend on the shoulder.

"Bullshit. We need all the help we can get right now. Thank you Kavvin. You are very much required to ensure we are successful. I've seen your skill." Felicity countered, giving Mark'Orr a death stare.

"Ok, let's get ready. Iron out our plan and who we must contact. Two days will fly by when we are having fun." Kavvin winked at Felicity.

6

PLANET: HOON

KAVVIN'S CABIN

"Catch," Kavvin called as he leant into a large wooden chest. Felicity caught the strange-looking laser pistol with cat-like reflexes.

"Fuck. How old is this thing?" She gave it a shake, hearing a few loose pieces rattle around inside the casing.

"Hey, gentle with that. Don't discriminate, it might be old but it's mighty. Kind of like me." He grinned as he looked over his shoulder at Felicity. She gave him her best deadpan expression. He quickly buried his head back in the chest to dig out more weapons.

"These beauties are from my old days with the Mercs." He held up a matching pair of silver engraved handles.

"What are they?" She stepped closer.

"Step back and I'll show you." She moved a few paces backwards and waited.

He flicked his wrists and two forearm-length beams of light erupted from the end of the silver.

"Oh fuck yes. I'll have those! You have this." Felicity offered the pistol back to Kavvin.

"Not a chance, young one. These are Alorean weapons, and two of my most prized possessions. They stay with me always."

"Ok what else you got in there?" She motioned to look into the chest. Kavvin retracted the light beams and shut the chest.

"A man's chest is a place of sanctity. Not to be rummaged in by others." He held his finger on the metal lock as it scanned him before it clicked, signalling it was secure.

The cabin door creaked open. Mark'Orr looked nervous as he stepped in, pushing the door closed behind him. The wind howled, as dry leaves spun in mini tornados outside.

"Hey, you ok?" Kavvin asked.

"Yeah, just hope this plan doesn't go to shit," He gruffed. "The weather is not a good omen." Felicity rolled her eyes at Mark'Orr.

"Oh come on. You know that omen stuff is bullshit. It all comes down to good planning and prep," Felicity chucked the pistol to him. "Here."

Mark'Orr fumbled, nearly dropping the pistol.

"Ah! fuck. Why'd you throw it to butter fingers over there?" Kavvin snapped at Felicity.

"Butterfingers?" Felicity snorted. "Brilliant. Mark'Orr

can have that, and I'll have something else from your magic chest over there," She put her hands on her hips expectantly.

"Fucksake. Fine. I'll find you something else. No peeking." Kavvin opened the biometric lock and began rummaging in the chest again. A moment later he closed the chest and tossed a weapon at Felicity.

"What the hell is this? Are you taking the actual fucking piss?" She held the small dagger out in front of her, not wanting to take ownership.

"Don't be ungrateful Felicity. It's an ugly trait." Kavvin smirked.

"Markyboy, let's swap." She offered the dagger to him and held out her other hand to receive the ancient pistol back. He laughed at her, a chuckle at first, but soon it became hysterical.

"No fucking way," He held the pistol away from her. "I'm better suited to something I can point and fire. You have better combat skills than me." Mark'Orr explained as he caught his breath.

"Ok, whatever." She slotted the dagger into her waistband. "We won't need weapons anyway. It's two and a half hours until the transfer. Kavvin, you said it's twenty minutes to get to the airfield. I think we should go now, and scout out a good place to hide out."

"Agreed. Here, you can wear this coat, Felicity." Kavvin chucked a camouflage coat at her. "And Mark'Orr, there is one on the hook there that should fit you, big man." He turned and grabbed some other items from a drawer in the unit under the window, shoving things in his pockets.

They pulled on coats, slotted their weapons into pockets and Mark'Orr grabbed his portable comms device. It was more than just for comms, it was a complete portable workstation. He had acquired many useful gadgets during his years on Hoon. None of it belonged to the Military or campus.

"Ok, head out." Kavvin held the door open as Felicity and Mark'Orr stepped out. He locked the door using biometrics.

They piled onto the small four-wheeler and headed deeper into the forest.

"Hey, you sure this is the way?" Felicity asked. Kavvin didn't bother responding as he manoeuvred through the thick bushes. He raised his hand in a thumbs up.

After what felt like an age, they stopped. Felicity checked the time on the wrist unit Kavvin gave her. Mark'Orr destroyed hers and his before they arrived at Kavvin's to ensure they couldn't be tracked.

"The airfield is just through those trees." Kavvin pointed in front of them.

"It's ten past six. The Segurian ship is due to arrive at just after eight." She looked up at the sky, the clouds were coming over and it was beginning to get dark. "Let's find our spot now and be ready." She marched ahead, barely a sound from her steps through the leaves on the ground. Kavvin smiled proudly and nudged Mark'Orr.

"Oi, you two stop clowning around. Hurry up, we

need to exit the trees carefully, in case they are patrolling."

They crouched low, gently pushing the branches aside of a thick leafy bush. The airfield quickly came into view.

A series of large hangars were set off to the side of a large expanse of hard compacted waste material which was the main landing zone. The ground was marked in flush LED lights, indicating different areas.

They shuffled through the tall grass, finding a convenient ditch near the edge of the landing zone. Felicity held up a hand motioning them to stop. She scanned the area.

A rustling noise had her turning to face Kavvin. She caught him mid-snack and stared him down. He retracted the snack and shoved it back into his pocket. Mark'Orr grinned.

"What? We have hours until they arrive anyway?" He whispered. Felicity rolled her eyes and turned back to the airfield.

"What the hell is going on there?" She pointed to the right. The other two shuffled up beside her to take a closer look.

"Oh fuck. Those are Segurians. Why are they loading a Hoon military ship?" Mark'Orr panicked. "Did we get the times wrong? Was it six twenty, not eight twenty?"

"Fuck." Felicity watched as the loading hatch began to close. A large netted box was secured in the cargo hold. A group of large, mean-looking Segurians shook hands with Shona as they boarded the ship. Shona and her crew turned and headed back for their own transport to take them back to campus.

"They're leaving!" She growled.

"I'm sorry. I fucked up." Mark'Orr groaned.

"None of us guessed it would be six and not eight. Don't worry. I have a plan. Follow me." Felicity went to stand, but was pulled back down by the bottom of her camp jacket.

"What the hell are you doing?" Kavvin scowled. "I came here to help you with getting them caught in the act. It's too late, we'll have to head back."

"BULLSHIT. I'm not letting Shona win. Not a fucking chance in hell. This is my chance to redeem myself and Mark'Orr. Nothing will stop me. I'm taking that shuttle and I'm going after them. Now, are you in or out?" She motioned to the small shuttle parked next to the hanger.

"Oh fuck no. You've got to be kidding me." Kavvin shuffled back.

"I'm not kidding. It's now or never. I know you must have had some experience with all your time on the Merc ships." She glanced back to the larger Hoon ship." They're taking off. Fuck it. I'll do it on my own."

Felicity stood and sprinted for the smaller shuttle. Smacking the entry button when she reached it. The ramp extended and she jumped inside. She scanned the inside to familiarise herself. She'd only had a few training sessions with the shuttles, and only on the basics.

"Fuck," She growled as she walked through the main

compartment and into the front section where the navigation seats were. She took a seat in the central position and started flicking on the main switches. It began whirring to life.

"Hey, shift over." Felicity jumped out of her skin as she heard Kavvin next to her. "What did I tell you about being aware of your surroundings?" He smirked. "Now hurry! Looks like we have company." Kavvin pushed Felicity into the seat beside the middle one. She glanced back as Mark'Orr closed the hatch.

"Fuck. We need to get out of here!" Mark'Orr shouted.

Felicity looked out the side window to see Shona Williams sprinting across the landing field, heels in her hands. Close behind her was Rex and a couple of others she didn't recognise.

"Shit. Lift us up Kavvin!" Felicity shouted.

"Buckle up, it's been many years since I've flown anything. I'm trying to override the security on this thing," Kavvin grumbled as he tapped several sequences on the panel in front of him. He stopped suddenly.

"What the hell!? Come on Kavvin!" Felicity urged.

"Hang on. I need to think."

"Seriously? This is no time to think!" She glanced out the window. The Superintendent was a mere hundred metres away. "Shit, how is that woman running so fast? I bet she's had GSET!"

Kavvin reached up, flicked a switch and then continued tapping in sequences. The shuttle juddered.

Felicity gripped the shoulder restraints of her safety belt. Just as Shona and her cronies made it to the shuttle it made a wobbly lift-off. Higher and higher they went. Felicity felt safe seeing Shona and her brother disappear into specks.

"Mark'Orr, we need to lock onto the other military ship that the Segurians have commandeered. We need to get to it before they reach their mother ship. Else we're fucked on many levels." Kavvin called out behind him.

"On it!" Mark'Orr responded. Within twenty seconds the visual display showed their position and the position of the Hoon military shuttle.

"Shit. That was fast. You're good boy," Kavvin whistled.

"You know it," Mark'Orr responded smugly.

"So what made you two stop being pussies hiding in the bushes and join me?"

"We knew you had no chance of getting this shuttle going. Couldn't see you caught by Shona and punished just to satisfy her anger at being made a fool of." Mark'Orr spoke quietly.

"Thanks, you two. You're right, I didn't know what I was doing with the shuttle. So how long until we reach them?"

"About thirty minutes give or take. They are bigger and heavier, with larger engines, but we are smaller, lighter and will soon catch up," Mark'Orr explained. "So, any bright ideas what we're going to do when we reach them?"

Felicity sat in silence for a moment before she responded. "First, you need to send a message to your contacts in Eskeron, urgently. Tell them about the GSET, the illegal transfer you decoded, the Superintendent's involvement, and that we are currently in pursuit of the Segurians who have commandeered a Hoon Military ship. When we reach the ship, we need to dock it. Somehow."

"Hang on just a minute. I'm not going onto a Segurian ship to be slaughtered." Mark'Orr objected. "And Kavvin here needs to keep the shuttle running."

Felicity nodded. "Yes, I figured that already. I will be going in."

"Hang on!" Mark'Orr was about to object, "SHIT!"

"What? It's not so bad, I have GSET in my blood now remember."

"No! We have a Hoon military ship on our tail. Kav, you better be good at evasive flying, they're trying to lock onto us."

"Oh, Markyboy you have no idea," He whooped as he spun the shuttle in a three-sixty corkscrew before levelling off. He glanced at Felicity and grinned. "Like that?"

"Not really. But if you think it will get them off our tail, then crack on."

"Seriously, could have given me some warning. Man with equipment back here remember!" Mark'Orr huffed as he gathered his things and strapped them down using velcro strips attached to the ledge next to his seat.

"A few minutes out from the Segurians now. I've sent a message to the Major General of the Eskeron Military. It has been some time since I contacted him, so not sure he remembers my parents or if he'll reply." Mark'Orr explained.

Felicity felt a jolt of nerves and excitement at stopping the Segurians, and therefore giving Shona and Rex what they deserved.

"Approaching their ship from the starboard side," Kavvin announced.

7

OUTER SPACE

APPROACHING SEGURIAN SHUTTLE

"Here, take these," Kavvin reached into his coat and handed Felicity the two metal light-swords.

"Ah Kavvin, no, you keep hold of those," Felicity unbuckled and stood.

"Seriously, have you always been this stubborn, girl? Just take the darn things. Hop over there, beat the shit out of them and then you can bring them back to me," He thrust them at her and she took them reluctantly.

"Felicity, we don't have a docking tunnel, how're you going to get across to their ship?" Mark'Orr asked.

"Well, we have anchors, yes? I remember that much from my lessons," Gunny stated. Mark'Orr nodded. "And I'm sure there must be some sort of emergency atmospheric protection suit?" Mark'Orr nodded again and pointed to the small cabinet to the side. "Well then, isn't it obvious? I'll jump across onto their ship."

"Only one small problem, dear Felicity," Mark'Orr

teased. "How are we going to get them to open their hatch into their airlock?"

"That's where you and Kavvin come in, dear Marky-boy. You'll use your excellent hacker skills and connect to their ship to take control." She winked. Mark'Orr laughed forgetting the seriousness of their situation for a second.

"Ok, we'll do our best. Never done anything like that before. Shit Major General has responded personally! He said they are too far out to get to us in time but are redirecting a ship from nearby. They'll be here within fifteen minutes. Can we wait for them?" He asked hopefully.

"No. We have to stop the Segurian ship from reaching their mothership and need to avoid the Military ship on our tail. We have to act now!" Kavvin shouted from his captain seat. "Felicity, suit up and get ready. Mark'Orr, how are we doing with linking to the Hoon ship?"

Felicity grabbed the suit and helmet, sliding into it, she clipped the helmet on and pressed the seal button on the shoulder. The suit sucked out excess air, leaving her in a form-fitting blue one-piece. She looked down and shook her head. A tracksuit was not the best idea to wear underneath, but she didn't have time to get undressed first. She strapped the weapons onto the built-in utility belt and pressed the button at the rear of the main compartment, it slid open onto a small airlock room. She entered and closed the door behind her. It sealed with a hiss. The shuttle juddered as it anchored to the larger ship.

"Ready, girl?" Kavvin called over the speakers in her helmet.

"Ready as I'll ever be."

"Go for it. Those fuckers have no idea what's about to enter their ship," Mark'Orr grinned.

The outer hatch slid open, revealing the black of space. Some distance, directly in front of her, was the hulking great Hoon military ship. From one of the small viewing windows, she could see a Segurian shouting and pointing at her. She grinned. She had years of anger saved up and ready to rain down on these poor fuckers like an anger-tsunami.

"Ok Felicity, see that red button above the door?" Kavvin's voice came over the speaker.

"Roger that."

"Press it!"

Felicity reached above the exit and slammed her palm on the button through the glove of her suit, thankful for her height. Most regular-sized people wouldn't be able to reach that button. She did wonder why it was so high and was about to comment about its stupid placement when two harpoon-like metal rods shot out towards the Hoon ship. They pierced the outer shell, causing the Hoon ship to immediately auto-repair, sealing the rods in place.

"Well, I'll be. So that's why the button isn't easy to reach." She laughed. Chains were attached to the ends of the rods, which anchored their shuttle to the ship, allowing some give.

Their shuttle juddered as it was hit by a laser cannon of the pursuing ship, which likely had Shona at the helm.

"Shields are up but don't know how long they'll last Felicity. You need to hurry. The Hoon military won't want to damage us too much, as they risk damaging the Segurian's ship and breaking whatever deal they have struck with them." Kavvin called.

"Or they might want to just get rid of all evidence and blow all of us to pieces?" Mark'Orr offered.

"Thanks for that Markyboy," Felicity shook her head. The airlock of the Hoon ship across from her opened.

"Space jumping. Whoever thought I'd be doing this in my fourth year at military school." She laughed as she attached a line to the chain above her.

"You ain't in school no more girl. Fast track to graduation and beyond." Kavvin laughed.

"Shit, you're telling me. Here goes." She leapt out of the shuttle, momentarily astounded at her weightlessness. She quickly focused on pulling herself across. Halfway there she jolted to a stop. She tugged on the safety line. "Shit it's jammed." She didn't even bother explaining what she was going to do. She knew time was of the essence. She unclipped the safety line, gripping the chain she swung herself like a torpedo into the airlock of the Hoon ship just as it closed shut.

"Fuck me, that was a close one. Can you hear me, boys?" She landed gracefully as the room depressurised.

"Loud and clear, you crazy assed fucker." Kavvin replied. "Opening the inner hatch now, be ready, I expect they're piling up to get at you. Remember your training, breath and let your body do its magic." She nodded at Kavvin's advice. The gravity of the situation was just sinking in.

"Fuck. Come on." She muttered to herself.

She pulled the light-swords from her belt, flicking them on. "Ready."

The door slid open revealing four Segurians crowding her exit. They suddenly all crashed in towards her as the ship bucked upward. Her mind flitted to her friends in the smaller shuttle under attack. She took advantage of the surprise jolt in the ship. She flicked her wrists, igniting the lasers. One in each hand. They glowed a glorious orange. At that moment she couldn't wait to slice through everything in her path.

She lunged as the Segurians tumbled in her direction, swiping along with her right arm, gutting two of them with ease. Red and green blood sprayed across her face as their entrails bubbled out from their abdomens.

In the same moment with her left light-sword she stabbed upwards as the Segurian fell forward. The laser sizzled straight through his eye socket and out the back of his skull.

She stood to face the fourth Segurian. Grinning.

"Felicity, you ok in there?" Mark'Orr called.

"Oh yes. These fucking swords are incredible." She replied as she stalked towards her final adversary.

"Who the fuck are you, bitch?" She could hear the slight waver in his voice. He was scared. *And so you should be, scum.* She growled at him and he jumped.

"I'm your worst fucking nightmare. I have nothing to lose and everything to gain." She stalked towards him.

He had no option but to charge her. He threw a punch. Felicity swung her wrist outwards blocking the punch, slicing his hand clean off with the laser. He screamed out in agony and in a last-ditch attempt, grabbed for the light-sword in Felicity's left hand. She allowed him to hold it, as she swung down with her right hand and chopped his other hand clean off at the forearm. He fell to his knees. She left him to bleed out, knowing it would be minutes.

"Felicity, report," Kavvin called.

"Four down. Leaving the airlock now," She responded clinically as she put the light swords in her belt.

"Head for the bridge, Felicity. I need you to find the manual override switch. Also, if you can try to keep a few of them alive, that would help us," Mark'Orr chimed in.

"Yes, Sirs."

"And Felicity? Be careful, this isn't a simulation," Mark'Orr warned.

"Shit, Markyboy, if you saw the blood dripping from me, you would see that I realise this isn't a game."

"Are you bleeding?" he asked, sounding panicked.

"Calm down. It's their blood. Not mine. Now shh, I need to focus." She peered out of the airlock. The walkway was clear. She turned left, towards the bridge.

She heard heavy steps behind her as she approached the sealed bridge door. Turning slowly, she was faced with a mountain of a Segurian.

"What the hell are you? Looks like you drink GSET for breakfast." She eyed him up. The Segurian grunted, casually stepping towards her.

"Shut it. You've caused enough trouble. What's a little girl like you doing on this ship? Playtime is over, whore." He lunged towards her with arms outstretched. His plates for hands angling towards her head.

His movements slowed down in her mind as he approached. His words cut through her, reminding her that assholes weren't just on Hoon, but everywhere. Felicity was thankful for the years of stretching and martial arts training she had done as she dropped into the splits. She poured all her energy into a double punch upwards, into the mountain's crotch. She felt his gonads disappear up into his body upon impact.

He gasped in a breath, eyes bulging and unable to speak before he fell to the deck.

"Shit. Didn't think it would be that easy. You deserved worse." She shook her head at the unconscious Segurian. *The bigger they are, the harder they fall*, she smirked.

"Did you face more Segurians?" Kavvin asked.

"One giant mother fucker. But all it took was a punch to the nuts and he's out."

"Oooh, that's gotta hurt." Kavvin sympathised. "Ok get to the bridge."

"I'm at the door. It's locked. Any ideas?" Felicity waited.

"Those light-swords can cut through metal," Kavvin suggested.

"On it." She pulled out a light sword, flicking it on with a quick motion. Touching the glowing orange tip to the metal of the door, sparks began to fly out as she applied more pressure. The ship juddered hard again, the light-sword jumped from her hand. Felicity pulled her arm away before the glowing blade dismembered her.

"Felicity, you're going to have to hurry. That Hoon military ship is trying to dock with us, I don't know how long I can evade them.

"Could have given me some warning. I nearly cut my fucking hand off. Gimme a sec." She responded as she picked the blade back up. She put her focus back on breaking into the bridge. She was nearly on the final cut to make a complete rectangular hole when she felt the barrel of a plasma pistol pressed against her neck. *Shit.*

"Got you now, little bitch. You're going to pay for that." The Segurians voice was strained, so she knew he was still in pain from her perfectly aimed double punch. It was the only time she would ever be glad of a male having big nuts.

"Kav. An evasive manoeuvre right about now would be really helpful," She spoke clearly and slowly.

"Felicity? Is everything ok?" Mark'Orr asked, before Kavvin chimed in.

"Coming right up milady," Kavvin said far too chirpily

as he pulled their shuttle in a fast downward motion, dragging the larger ship down on one side.

Felicity was prepared, but the Segurian was not. He stumbled, hitting his back against the opposite wall a few paces away. Before she could get to him, he fired a series of shots her way. She dropped to the ground, and rolled towards him, slicing out with the light sword. He toppled over, but his feet remained in place, severed at the ankle. He screamed, writhing on the floor as a loud hissing noise came from behind her head.

"Uh guys, I think we have a problem," Felicity called to her friends. Warning sirens in the ship began to blare out, along with flashing red lights.

"You don't think? Has it taken you this bloody long to figure that out?" Kavvin snapped back.

"No, the big bastard shot holes through the side of the ship. If we want to keep some of these bastards alive. I'll need to plug them quickly." She was glad to have her suit on now, even if it was a ridiculous-looking blue thing.

"Ok, you've got to get into the bridge. There's a repair kit. Be careful, you will be exposed when you enter." Mark'Orr advised.

Felicity ignored the screams from the footless Segurian as she finished cutting her way through the bridge doorway. She stepped back and kicked the panel. It flew inwards. She heard a cry from inside the bridge. Holding the light sword out in front of her she stepped through the hole.

The panel she had kicked in, had flown across the

bridge, stabbing the back of a chair. A Segurian sat in the chair groaning, as another tried to figure out how badly his captain had been hurt.

"Sit the fuck down," She shouted to the one trying to help. The Segurian turned to Felicity, snarling. She was a weedy-looking female but looked like she'd had a tough life by the many scars across her face.

The female ran at her, screaming. She clotheslined the crazy Segurian by the neck, before kneeling with the light sword hovering just above her face.

"See this? It just cut through that door. Want it through your head? No? Go sit the fuck down."

Felicity must have looked foreboding, covered in blood, having just cut through the bridge door single-handedly. The female crawled back to her seat. Felicity followed. Strapping her in tightly. The other Segurian, an older male, seemed to be falling in and out of consciousness, so she focussed on securing the female by grabbing a set of restraints from another chair and buckling the Segurian in. When she was satisfied the female wouldn't escape she leant towards her.

"This ship is decompressing. If you want to continue breathing oxygen, I suggest you sit still while I fix it." She walked towards the back of the bridge.

"Ok, I'm in. Where is the patch kit and where is the override switch?"

"Patch kit first, if we want to keep a few of our witnesses alive. There should be a bank of lockers at the back. The engineering section is always the second locker in, straight after the medical locker. It should be in a yellow case."

Felicity pulled the first locker open and was pleased to see it was the first aid items. She opened the second, but couldn't see a yellow case. Tools were strapped to the sides of the locker, on the shelf below was a purple case and on the shelf above was a blue case. "Fuck. No yellow case. Checking the other lockers." She scrambled to open the remaining three lockers, but couldn't find a yellow case, so she returned to the second locker. Pulling out the blue case, she popped the lid but found only strange-looking fuses and plugs connected to cables. She tossed it on the floor and grabbed the purple case. Popping the lid, she found a series of different-sized metal patches and tubes of some type of epoxy resin.

"Gotcha! By the way, it was in a fucking purple case. Have you got some sort of lonely man's colour blindness?" She marched out to the hall with the case in hand. Stepping over the large Segurian, who had passed out from loss of blood, or possibly expired, she reached the four holes in the wall of the ship.

"Ok, I'm here. I'm guessing I just slap one of these things on with some of the stuff from the tube?"

"Considering I can't see what you're talking about, a bit of a description wouldn't go amiss," Kavvin replied. Felicity sighed audibly.

"Oxygen running low. No time! Metal patches and tubes of some stuff. What next?"

"Ah yes, open the tube, apply it liberally to the patch and stick to the hole, hold on for a few seconds."

"Ok, gimme a sec."

"Hang on. Be careful you don't get it on your suit. It is strong shit, it will burn through that material."

"Got it." Felicity put the case on the deck and pulled out four patches and laid them on the inside lid of the case. She opened a tube, piercing the seal.

Squeezing the tube, a blue stretchy gel emerged. She smeared it onto the patch, keeping her fingers to the edges. Pushing the patch onto the hole, she pressed down firmly before repeating this for the other three holes.

"Ok holes fixed. Where's this override switch?"

"FELICITY! BRACE! INCOMING FIRE!" Mark'Orr shouted over the comms. A crackling noise followed, indicating she had lost connection. Out in the walkway, there wasn't much to grab onto. Before she could get into the bridge, the whole shuttle jolted up, before going into a sickening spin. She heard the groan and snap of the metal restraints that had been keeping the smaller shuttle tethered to the larger one.

The force of the spinning had Felicity stuck to the ceiling. She stretched her arms and legs out to brace against the walls on each side as the ship was stuck in an increasingly fast death roll. She knew she didn't have long before she would pass out. As that thought crossed her mind, images of her real parents came to her. Parents who had loved her, who had been killed in action, fighting for worthy causes. If she were to die now, she knew she'd have died for a worthy cause. And killing some bastard sexist Segurians along the way only sweetened the deal. Stars flickered in her vision as she tried to focus on the dead Segurian who was pressed to the floor below her. She felt a pain in her temple before everything went black.

8

OUTER SPACE
SEGURIAN SHUTTLE

"Ms Fairwether? Felicity?" An unfamiliar voice sounded distant in Felicity's mind. She cracked an eye open but she could only see bright lights and squeezed her eye shut.

"Beriss, turn that light off." The voice called. "Felicity? Can you hear me?"

She groaned as she tried to open her eyes again slowly. No blinding lights. She opened them further. The scene in front of her brought her back to reality. A uniformed officer crouched over her in the walkway of the Hoon Military ship, as she lay sprawled on the floor. She realised her helmet was now missing.

"What's going on? Are Mark'Orr and Kavvin ok?" She sat up quickly and instantly regretted it.

"Ms Fairwether. We need you to come with us. Can you stand?"

The avoidance of the question and the formal tone of the female officer told her enough. Emotion welled inside her, but she tamped it down. She wouldn't show weakness to anyone. Not ever again. Felicity got up slowly, refusing the offer of assistance from the officer. She was marched off the ship, through a docking tunnel, straight onto an Eskeron Military ship, where she was led to a small cabin.

"You can make yourself comfortable in here. When they are ready for you, I will be back." She nodded formally before exiting. The door slid closed behind her, followed by an audible click, telling her she was locked in there.

Fuck. This is it. I'm a prisoner. Shona must have gotten to them. She'll pin everything she can on me. I'm fucked. She sat down on the bunk and held her head in her hands. She flopped to her side, curling into herself before passing out from exhaustion.

Distant voices floated in her mind before she realised they were coming from outside the door. She had been sleeping for what felt like a year. The door unlocked with a click, before it slid open. The same serious female officer stood in the entrance.

"I hope you were able to get some rest?" She asked, clearly trying to sound kind, but it came across as very formal. Felicity no longer had the patience for niceties or silly chit-chat.

"I did close my eyes for some time. Can you tell me what's going on now?" She tried again.

"I think it's best if you follow me please," She stepped out of the room and waited for Felicity to obey.

Felicity had respect for the Eskeron services. Her father was after all an Eskeronion. She dutifully exited the room and followed the officer down a hall and out of the ship into a waiting transport shuttle. *Fuck, we're on Eskeron.* A sliver of excitement passed through her. Felicity knew this officer wouldn't tell her anything so she didn't bother prying. The shuttle took them to a side entrance of the Military base, into the medical wing.

"Just through here please." The officer walked fast, but with Felicity's long legs she kept up easily. They entered a small medical room with a privacy screen.

"There is a shower cubicle and some fatigues for you to put on behind the screen. Please clean yourself up and I will be back in ten minutes." She left, locking the door behind her again, confirming to Felicity that she was a prisoner.

She peeled off the blue space suit, which was caked in dry blood from various Segurians. Some had been from Claghua, others from Hoon and other far-reaching places.

She rinsed the sweat and grime from her face, enjoying the simple feeling of hot water cleansing her. Ensuring she was on time, she towelled down and slipped on the uniform and boots. She guessed they had pulled her record already, as they had gotten her clothing size correct.

The door opened without a knock. The officer stepped back out, signalling for Felicity to follow once more.

Through corridors and over suspended walkways, they continued until they entered a much more formal building. This was where the senior officers would meet and discuss matters surrounding Eskeron and partnering planets, and the wider Hyperion System.

Large opulent lighting reflected off the polished black floors in the lobby. The officer ushered Felicity through a set of double doors, down a hallway and into another room.

This room was simple, with a black glossy table and two chairs on each side. Mirrors filled the room.

Felicity knew instantly that this was an interrogation room. A nicer one than she had ever seen in her studies on campus, but nevertheless it was still a room to grill her in. She tried to remember anything she had been taught about interrogation techniques but quickly remembered that she had nothing to hide. She had acted on behalf of Hoon and Eskeron when they tried to stop the Segurians.

"Please, take a seat. Our intelligence officer will be in shortly to speak with you." She left the room, closing the door.

Within minutes, a short, serious-looking man entered in full Eskeron Military uniform.

"Ms Fairwether. May I call you Felicity?"

"I'd rather just Ms Fairwether please." She replied coldly. The officer looked at her with surprise but continued as he took a seat.

"Very well. Ms Fairwether, can you give us a detailed account of what happened?"

"Where shall I begin?"

"How about from a week ago."

✹

After an hour of briefing shorty on what had happened, and whoever else was behind the mirrored wall. She was given a cup of water and a ration bar. He left her in the room for a while longer.

She began doubting herself. *Have I said something wrong? Did I mention anything about the attack in the forest?* Before she could analyse it any further, the female officer entered the room.

"Ok, it's time. You are requested to have an audience with the Major General. He doesn't like to be kept waiting." She marched out. Felicity stood, a feeling of dread washed over her. She followed the female officer once more, back along the corridor, into the lobby.

They approached large glass double doors, which opened when the officer scanned her face. They stood waiting for the glass doors to close behind them. When they clicked shut, there was a distinct difference between this area and the lobby with its polished floors. The plush carpets and wooden panelled walls gave a soft muted feel to the windowless space. The smell of wood preserver and old but well-kept carpet captured the long history this place held. Felicity was sure her father and mother would have come here at some point. She cast that silly, useless thought aside and focused on her judgement with the Major General and other Eskeron Military leaders.

Felicity glanced at the traditional old-world style paintings of past generals hung neatly on the panelled walls. She had hoped to climb the ranks, to make a difference. All that was ruined now. She followed the officer through a smaller wooden door into an antechamber. An armed guard stood at the door and nodded to the officer as he opened the door to let her pass. As Felicity passed him he smiled and nodded. She knew that was not protocol. *What the hell? Is this guy for real?* She averted her gaze, looking at the officer in front of her as she passed the guard.

They entered a large courtroom with crescent-tiered seating. Five levels down, in the centre of the room, a hip-height polished wooden barricade surrounded a raised dais, with a long elegant desk, where three highly ranked officials sat. They watched her as she made her way down the steps.

Felicity glanced around the room quickly. Most of the seats were empty, apart from a few uniformed members on the other side on the second tier up. *Shit. No audience, this is just a verdict. No chance to plead my case.*

The officer pointed her to a standing spot, centrally

aligned with the dais, just outside of the wooden barricade.

Felicity saluted, standing tall, even though she felt like there was no point. These men deserved respect.

"Felicity Aurora Fairwether. At ease." The man sitting in the middle requested. His firm voice filled the room without the need for any amplifier. His uniform told her he was the Sergeant General. Felicity released her salute, but stood straight, maintaining relaxed eye contact evenly spread across her three seniors.

"We have brought you here for sentencing. Intelligence specialist lecturer, Mark'Orr Derilin, of Hoon Military, notified us of events occurring yesterday. We have taken evidence from all living sources and taken into account the ships and Hoon equipment involved in the incident."

Felicity braced herself.

"There are multiple counts of damage to Hoon Military property, which is a supporting arm of the Eskeron Military. There is the theft of a Hoon Military Shuttle and use of illegal weapons by untrained, underage personnel."

Felicity gulped. *Shit. Kavvin's light swords. Ah fuck.*

"What do you plead to the charges against you?" He asked her seriously. She didn't have a leg to stand on. As the only survivor of the mission, it was her word against Shona's.

"Guilty, sir." She knew not to speak out, it had been

drilled into them from young. The general banged his gavel once.

"A punishment suited to these crimes would be a permanent stay on Nightforge prison on the edges of the Hyperion System."

"However. There is further evidence to offset against these crimes." The General nodded to the guard at a door to the side. The guard left the room, and seconds later he returned, with two people following. The lights shining in Felicity's eyes blocked her from seeing who it was. When the group came closer, it took all of Felicity's strength to continue standing. She wanted to shout out and cry, but she knew she had to maintain her stance.

Mark'Orr nodded to her as he hobbled along, maintaining a solemn expression. Kavvin was at his side helping him, he had no such qualms about freely smiling as he grinned up at Felicity and winked. The guard ushered them to sit, given their injuries. She was too far from them to whisper, and it would have shown disrespect to the General.

"After questioning all sources independently, and cross-referencing this with our own investigations, using some of our best, I would like to thank all three of you for your bravery. Your stupidity paid off on this occasion, and you somehow drew in all connected parties to one place at one time. Whether this was planned or whether it was a coincidence, one thing's for sure, it was damn good timing. On behalf of the Eskeron Military, we would like to thank the three of you for putting your lives at risk to stop the transfer of GSET to Segurian hands. It has highlighted some clear leaks in our system, which we are currently rectifying as we speak."

Felicity could well imagine what they meant by 'rectifying'. Someone caught stealing large shipments of GSET and supplying it to Shona on Hoon to sell on would mean not just the end of their career, but the end of their life.

"I have a proposal to make to the three of you now." The General continued. "Mark'Orr, you are top of your field in Intelligence, I would hate to see that go to waste out on Hoon. Will you accept the invitation to join our ranks here on Eskeron?" The General was not about to let them take their time thinking about it. When someone like him made a personal offer like that, if you didn't accept, you may as well go find a job on Nova X space station cleaning toilets.

Mark'Orr winced as he stood to attention, straightening to his full height. "Sir. It would be my honour to join the Eskeron forces. Thank you for the opportunity." He nodded before Kavvin helped him to take a seat. Felicity watched the exchange, worried about her friend's injuries.

The General fixed his gaze on Felicity. "Ms Fairwether, how it is that your friends here are badly injured from the missile explosion, yet you were stuck in a death roll heading into space, and there is not a scratch on you?"

"Sir. There was a situation some weeks ago." She didn't want to go into detail, especially not in this environment. She had sworn to never talk about what happened again. It just brought up more bad memories from her adoptive father's cruel treatment of her too. Her mother had always been too drunk to realise what was going on.

"I was fatally wounded. A distant friend of a friend gave me a dose of GSET. It saved my life, Sir." She had just stretched the truth quite a lot with that statement.

"I see. And this friend? Care to divulge any more?"

"Sir, I was unconscious, so I am unable to give any further details." She could see from the corner of her eye, Kavvin relax slightly. She had no doubts that the General knew exactly who gave her the GSET. But if she didn't say it, and he didn't press for any more information, then all was good.

"Well, Ms Fairwether, it was very lucky indeed that this unknown source had an illegal dose of GSET on hand. We will ensure there are no more leaks from our supply. I have pulled your records. An impressive set of achievements, given your age, and prior to this GSET shot too. I would like to offer you a place in our military on Eskeron too. At your age, normally you would go into the rank of Private. But taking into account the mission you have cracked, which, might I add, is a case that some of our own have been trying to figure out for some time without success, I will put you in as Corporal. I know you will prove yourself worthy. You are young, but I can see you have the balls to command a team. Do you accept?"

Felicity saluted proudly, "Yes, Sir. Thank you, Sir." She swallowed down the lump in her throat.

"Lastly, a rarity for us. Kavvin Petheus, of Alorea. Dare I ask how you found yourself caught up in all of this?"

Kavvin stood proudly, his Alorean cockiness shining through. "Sir, my mother was from Hoon. I moved back from Alorea with her when I came of age. I worked various jobs over the years but finally settled on Hoon. I have known Mark'Orr for many years. He is a good friend."

The General nodded. "And Kavvin, what skills do you possess and do you think you could offer anything to the Eskeron Military?"

"Sir, I do not believe I have skills that would assist you in the military. I have a small plot and a cabin, where I would like to see out my days quietly. I hope this does not offend you?"

"Remember Kavvin, we know much more than you possibly realise. You most certainly do possess some skills that we may find of use, but I do respect your wishes after your assistance in bringing down the illegal GSET trade. How about, if we need you, we can call upon you?"

Kavvin bowed, "Yes Sir, I believe that is something I can agree to."

"Excellent. Felicity, the briefing starts tomorrow. I

would like to catch up with you more to discuss the matter of your adoptive parents and requesting to sign you over to us. Kavvin, we will arrange your transport in the next hour to return to Hoon. Officer Reed will have some refreshments arranged and you can say your farewells in private. I will see you after that, Felicity." He stood and left the courtroom, followed by his two assistants.

Officer Reed approached. "If you would follow me, there is a lunch room prepared for you." She marched towards the exit. Felicity went to the other side of Mark'Orr to help him.

"I thought…" she blinked away the tears that threatened to fall.

"We know. We thought the same about you. They wouldn't tell us anything. We made it though. You did it, Felicity." He squeezed her shoulder as they hobbled along to the exit.

"I wish you could have seen it. Those light swords. Oh shit, Kavvin. The light swords. When I woke up, they'd taken them. Let me speak to the General. I need to get them back for you."

"Ah, it's ok, Felicity." Kavvin nodded. "They must have put two and two together when they identified the weapons as Alorean. They asked if they were mine. I admitted that they were. They said they'll lock them away and will send them to me if the General agrees. It's out of our hands." He shrugged with his left shoulder, as his right was currently tucked under Mark'Orrs arm.

"By the way, there's surveillance on all military ships. I wouldn't be surprised if they've already reviewed it," Mark'Orr advised.

The guard held the door open for them as they walked out, and were guided into another side room. The smell of fresh bread, coffee and fruits filled their nostrils as their eyes took in the glorious sight. The trio suddenly remembered just how hungry they were.

"Here we are. Enjoy. You have one hour before Kavvin's shuttle leaves and the General wants a second meet with you Ms Fairwether." Felicity nodded, grateful that the officer had gotten the memo to not call her by her first name. The officer left the room, and Felicity waited for the telltale click of the lock, which never came. She smiled.

"We aren't prisoners anymore boys." She stuffed her mouth with a pastry. "So that footage. Wonder if we can get hold of it?…" She grinned.

END….

SEVEN YEARS LATER

PLANET: ESKERON

So now you know. I've worked my ass off for the Eskeron Military over the past seven years. I've been thrown in the deep end, waded through mud up to my waist in alien jungles as blood-sucking critters feasted on me. I've intercepted suicide bombers who were trying to blow up Nova X space station and fought against Kara'kuan fighters on Duplo V.

The General has promoted me each time for my achievements. But I hadn't expected his next move. He promoted me to Master Gunnery Sergeant, to run a team on specialist missions. This is where it got fun, I didn't want to work with pissants and newbies. I wanted the best of the best in my squad. The General allowed me to create my own handpicked team of elite soldiers. Much to the jealousy and frustration of other Sergeants. Fuck 'em. They weren't the ones being asked to walk through the fires of hell and still get back, intact, and ready for the next mission.

I picked the most promising men and women. I had thirty-five in total. Over the following year, they either didn't cut the mustard or they just couldn't take the pace. They got kicked.

I'm now left with the cream of the crop. Fifteen of the very best. I train these boys hard, and they're always ready for more. Onwards and upwards. Cobras all the way.

Catch you on the flip side.

Gunny - yeah that's my name.

HELLO!

This was such a fun story to write. Gunny is an interesting character, who appears in the series 'The Emiliana Chronicles'. The series is based in the Hyperion System, as are all of my Sci-Fi books. You can grab them here!

I'll be writing some more Novellas based on other characters from the main series, as each of them have their own history and background which I'd love to share.

The Emiliana Chronicles is a fast, action-packed Space Opera, with plenty of creative cussing. I am also currently writing a new series based on Klatu, in the Hyperion System - about a hacker who gets herself into all sorts of trouble!

An extra special thanks to AJ Rawlinson (The big daddio, Papa Rawlinson), for your input into the character that is Gunny. You will be forever missed.

And thank you again readers!

I hope you enjoy the next books in the series as much as I did writing them.

JR

x

ONE LAST THING...

If you enjoyed this book, I would bloody love it if you left me a little review on Amazon here!

Thanks again for your support!

JR

Printed in Dunstable, United Kingdom